For Frances, the coolest cat we know. Thank you for bringing this book to life.
Love, Kate and Lauren

Farrar Straus Giroux Books for Young Readers
175 Fifth Avenue, New York 10010

Text copyright © 2013 by Kate Banks
Pictures copyright © 2013 by Lauren Castillo
All rights reserved
Color separations by Bright Arts (H.K.) Ltd.
Printed in China by South China Printing Co. Ltd.,
Dongguan City, Guangdong Province
Designed by Jay Colvin
First edition, 2013
3 5 7 9 10 8 6 4 2

mackids.com

Library of Congress Cataloging-in-Publication Data
Banks, Kate, 1960–
    City cat / Kate Banks ; pictures by Lauren Castillo. — First edition.
        pages   cm
    Summary: An easy-to-read book about a globe-trotting cat that crosses paths with a
vacationing family in the great cities of Europe. Includes facts about the cities.
    ISBN 978-0-374-31321-0 (hardcover)
    [1. Voyages and travels—Fiction.   2. Cats—Fiction.   3. Europe—Fiction.]
    I. Castillo, Lauren, illustrator.   II. Title.

PZ7.B22594Cit 2013
[E]—dc23
                                                                        2012046729

Farrar Straus Giroux Books for Young Readers may be purchased for business or
promotional use. For information on bulk purchases please contact Macmillan
Corporate and Premium Sales Department at (800) 221-7945 x5442 or by email at
specialmarkets@macmillan.com.

CITY CAT

Kate Banks   Pictures by Lauren Castillo

Frances Foster Books

Farrar Straus Giroux

New York

Wake up, City Cat. It's dawn.
Watch the day put clothing on in city colors,
brown, black, rust, and gray.

City Cat heads for the street.
Sprinting, striding City Cat.

City Cat scales ragged walls.
She romps through ruins set in stone.
Then tiptoes through a sacred space
and cuddles in a hidden place
where she won't be found.

Wheels a-whirring, cat a-purring,
daring, wayfaring City Cat.
Where are you going, City Cat?

Dancing, prancing City Cat, waltzing past a French café.
She bathes herself around midday
underneath a fountain's spray.

City Cat, lured by smells of fresh-caught fish,
lurks around the city port.
She sits on piers with perked-up ears
and gazes out to sea.
The waves, they tumble, rise, and rumble,
beckoning City Cat.

Floating, boating City Cat.
Where are you drifting, City Cat?

City Cat slinks through market stalls,
where vendors sell their wares.
She pounces, prances, rolls around,
and disappears without a sound.

Oh, City Cat, nimble, agile City Cat arched like an arrow's willful bow.
She leaps from rooftops overhead
and makes a bed in terrace pots,
or naps in city parking lots.

Humming, drumming City Cat. Ssh!
Don't wake that City Cat.

City Cat, strutting down the boulevards,
taking in the city sights.
The skyline, pulsing, bathed in light.
An obelisk, a graceful arch,
a gilded bridge, a sprawling park.

She folds her paws and drops her head
and settles on a gargoyle's bed,
until wakened by a gentle rain.
She heeds the call of the midnight train.

Globe-trotting, train-spotting City Cat.
Where are you going, City Cat?

City Cat is on the run from the morning mist
and the baffled sun hidden by the fog.
She squints into a smoky sky
and sees a tower rising high.

City Cat stalks city birds, snarling, scratching City Cat.
Green eyes slanting, sitting proud,
she joins the starlings' evening dance.
Then in a trance she watches
the Changing of the Guard.

Windward, wayward City Cat.
Where are you going, City Cat?

Swaying, playing City Cat
mimics the tall ships' blowing masts.
Dazzled by a riverboat,
she stops to groom her satin coat
then hops on board and floats farther out to sea.

Rollicking, frolicking City Cat.
Tweaks her nose and wets her feet.
She searches for a bite to eat
then curls among the evening post, happy to have found a host.

Hustling, bustling City Cat.
Where are you going, City Cat?

Oh, City Cat, gallivanting City Cat,
circles under angel's wings
and listens to the city sing
its spinning wheels and merry crowds.

City Cat, waving her tail like a magic wand,
hears a clock chime overhead
and stops to watch a couple wed.

City Cat, where are you going, City Cat?

City Cat, marching through the narrow streets,
trots across the Bridge of Sighs
then taunts the pigeons in the square,
wishing for a mask to wear.

Masquerading City Cat,
serenading birds and bats.
Making mischief, chasing rats,
bold and brazen City Cat.

Careful now, don't make a sound. City Cat is homeward bound.
Wedged between two leather bags stamped with stickers of country flags,
she licks her fur and takes a nap
on a well-worn city map.
And when she wakes she's home again.

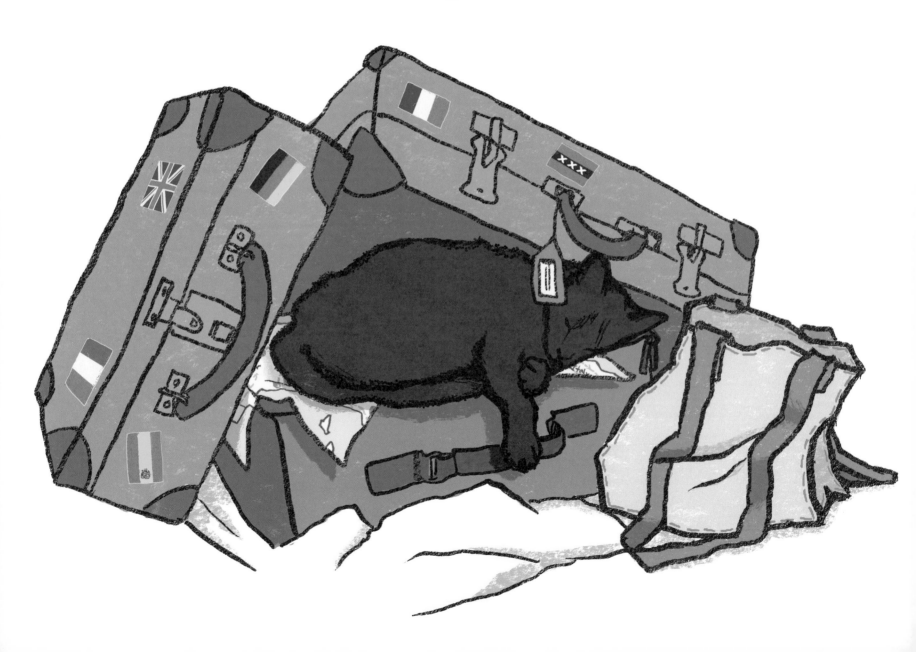

Tonight she'll sleep far from harm,
curled up in a statue's arm,
and dream of blinking city lights,
city travelers, and city nights.

Not far away, tucked in bed,
a little boy will turn his head
and dream of blinking city lights,
city cats, and city nights.

Barcelona, Spain: Every neighborhood in Barcelona has its own outdoor markets, which sell everything from vegetables, olives, and cheese to fish and flowers.

Casa Batlló, nicknamed House of Bones, was built in 1877 and later transformed by Antoni Gaudí. It is known for its mosaic tiling and flowing shapes. The Spanish word for cat is *gato*. The Catalan word is *gat*.

Rome, Italy: The Colosseum, completed in AD 80, was the largest amphitheater ever built in the Roman Empire. Today, over two hundred stray cats live rent-free at the Colosseum and are protected by Roman law. The Italian word for cat is *gatto*.

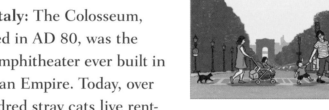

Paris, France: The Arc de Triomphe was commissioned in 1806 after Napoleon's victory at Austerlitz. Beneath the arch is the Tomb of the Unknown Soldier, honoring men who died in World War I and were never identified.

Marseille, France: The monumental Castellane Fountain in Place Castellane is a popular gathering spot in Marseille, the largest commercial port in France. It was sculpted in marble by André-Joseph Allar and was presented to the city in 1911. It depicts the journey of the Rhône River from its source, in Switzerland, to the Mediterranean Sea. The French word for cat is *chat*.

Notre Dame Cathedral is the spiritual heart of the French capital. Begun in 1163, it is considered one of the finest examples of French Gothic architecture. The largest bell in the towers weighs over 28,000 pounds; the gargoyles serve as drainpipes as well as decorations.

The black cat depicted in the lithograph *Le Chat Noir* (The Black Cat), by Théophile Steinlen, is a famous symbol of the city and can be found on souvenirs ranging from posters to mugs to umbrella stands.

London, England: Big Ben is the nickname for the clock and tower at the north end of Westminster Palace. It holds the largest four-faced chiming clock in the world. Completed in 1859, the clock is famous for its reliability.

Buckingham Palace has been the official London home of British sovereigns since 1837. It has 775 rooms. The royal family prefers dogs, so there are no cats in residence at the palace.

Amsterdam, the Netherlands: Known as the Venice of the North, Amsterdam boasts more than sixty miles of canals and more than twelve hundred bridges, most of which were built during the city's golden age in the seventeenth century.

The Catboat, a houseboat in Amsterdam's canal belt, is a sanctuary for stray cats. The Dutch word for cat is *kat*.

Munich, Germany: The Angel of Peace, whose stone foundation was laid in 1896, is a monument to the twenty-five peaceful years after the Franco-Prussian War.

The Glockenspiel dates from 1907 and is part of the New Town Hall in Marienplatz, in the heart of Munich. When it chimes, its thirty-two life-size figures reenact two stories from the sixteenth century. The German word for cat is *Katze*.

Venice, Italy: The Bridge of Sighs, built in 1602 by Antonio Contino, passes over the Rio di Palazzo. Prisoners crossed over the covered bridge on their way to interrogation rooms in the Doge's Palace.

St. Mark's Square is the principal public square of Venice. Located at one of the lowest points in the city, the square can flood quickly when rains are heavy or a storm blows in off the Adriatic Sea. The city of Venice has a big cat, the winged Lion of Saint Mark, as its mascot.